Pirates Aren't Afraid of the Dark!

For my big brother, Jonah.
Thanks for letting me share your flat.
~ M. P. T.

For Brian and Ivy, my lovely in-laws
~ A. E.

Originally published in Great Britain in 2014 by Little Tiger Press

ISBN 978-0-545-92532-7

12 11 10 9 8 7 6 5 4 3 2 1   15 16 17 18 19 20/0

Printed in the U.S.A.   40

First Scholastic printing, October 2015

Pirates Aren't Afraid of the Dark!

of the Dark!

by Maudie Powell-Tuck • Illustrated by Alison Edgson

SCHOLASTIC INC.

"Look, Parrot!" said Jack.
"I've painted a pirate flag!"
Jack had built a pirate tent in the
backyard and Mommy was going to
let him sleep in it all night long.
He couldn't wait.

"Can I stay in your pirate tent tonight?"
asked his sister, Lily, peeking in.
"No way!" Jack snorted.
"Why not?" said Lily.
"It will be spooky and there
will be scary sea monsters,"
said Jack. "Pirates aren't
afraid of the dark—
but fairies are!"

Jack stomped off to the pool.
He was playing pirates with his
boats when Lily raced over.
"Fairy ahoy!" she cried.

SPLASH!

"Fairies can't be pirates!"
grumbled Jack. "Leave me
alone!" And he sloshed back to
the house to dry off.

But Lily wouldn't go away. When Jack got back to his tent, there she was!

"Look, we're having a pirate tea party," she said. "Please, please, please can I stay with you in the pirate tent tonight?"

"Pirates *don't* have tea parties!" shouted Jack. "This is *my* tent, *my* toys, and *my* sleepover. No fairies allowed!"

Lily's wings drooped. With a sniff, she trudged away, dragging her wand behind her.

Outside, the sun dipped in the sky, and it grew dark. But Jack didn't mind one bit.

First, he made funny shadows with his flashlight. Then he read Parrot a scary story about a giant octopus.

Suddenly . . .

flicker – flicker – pop!

. . . the flashlight went out!

"Pirates aren't afraid of the dark," said Jack with a shiver.

Rustle, rustle, rustle...

"Who's there?" Jack squeaked.

Rustle, rustle...THUMP!

Something was inside the tent!

"It's the giant octopus!"
yelled Jack.

"Aargh!" cried Lily, leaping out.
"I'm Captain Fairydust, and I've come
to steal your ship. Walk the plank
or I'll turn you into a frog!"

"You're no match for Captain Growlyboots," said Jack, reaching for his sword.

He swished it through the air, then grabbed Lily's wand. "Prepare to be froggified!" he cried.

But Lily had gone quiet.

"Shh!" she whispered. "There's something outside."

Slowly, they looked out of the tent.

Rustle, rustle, rustle...

A big, black shape was coming toward them.

"What if it's a scary sea monster?" trembled Lily.

Rustle, rustle, rustle...

It was getting closer and closer.

"Hold my hand," whispered Jack.

"We'll zap it with your wand.

One, two, three . . . ."

"Monsters beware!" they
yelled. "Pirates aren't afraid of
the dark!"

"Of course they're not," said Mommy.
"But I've brought a special pirate
lantern just in case."

"Pirates always sleep with a night-light,"
nodded Captain Growlyboots.

"Do pirates like midnight feasts, too?"
smiled Mommy.

"Yes, please!" said Captain Fairydust, and
they sipped cocoa under the twinkling stars
until it was well past a pirate's bedtime.

"Tell me a story," said Lily as they snuggled into bed.

"Once," began Jack, "there were two pirates."

"What were their names?" yawned Lily.

"Captain Growlyboots and Captain Fairydust,"
said Jack, "and they were the bravest
brother and sister to sail the seven seas."

And Jack told Lily
swashbuckling story after
story until they both fell
fast asleep.